As the Publishers Weekly s... book jacket, this baby clearly has a mind of her own — Maybe she/he? will be more cooperative from here on out ???

Best Wishes — Mom

Aug. 1979

BABY

by Fran Manushkin   Pictures by Ronald Himler

Harper & Row, Publishers   New York   Evanston   San Francisco   London

BABY
Text copyright © 1972 by Frances Manushkin
Pictures copyright © 1972 by Ronald Himler

Library of Congress Catalog Card Number: 78-183159
Trade Standard Book Number 06-024061-X
Harpercrest Standard Book Number 06-024062-8

For my mother and father,
and for Marcel Perlman,
and Ezra Jack,
with love.

Mrs. Tracy was growing a baby.
She fed the baby very carefully.

For breakfast she gave the baby
milk, soft-boiled eggs,
and good raisin toast.

"Do you like your food?" she asked.
And from deep inside her,
Baby would say, "Ummm."

After breakfast, Mrs. Tracy would go
into a sunny room and paint.

She would put red, blue,
and every other color on paper
and paint them into lovely shapes.

Then she would tell Baby about them.
"Do you like your pictures?" she asked.
And Baby would say, "Ummm."

The days went by pleasantly,
until one day when Mrs. Tracy took Baby
for a walk in the woods.

"Baby, there are so many
little yellow flowers.
When you are born,
you will see them for yourself."

"I don't want to be born," said Baby.
"Oh yes, you must be born!"
said Mrs. Tracy.

"I am staying right here,"
insisted Baby.
Mrs. Tracy started to cry.
"What shall I do?" she wondered.

All she could do was go home.

When her children
came home from school,
she told them about Baby.
"We know how to make Baby come out,"
they said.

Laura put her head
against her mother's stomach.
"Baby," she asked, "can you hear me?"
"Yes," said Baby.

"COME OUT!" Laura yelled
as loud as she could.
"Waaaaa," cried Baby, "I won't.
You scared me."

Craig put his head
against his mother's stomach.
"Baby," he asked, "can you hear me?"
"Yes," said Baby.

"Come out, and I'll give you a nickel!"
he yelled.
"Waaaaa," cried Baby,
"I don't know what a nickel is,
and I won't come out."

Mrs. Tracy's mother came over.
She put her head
against her daughter's stomach.

"Baby, can you hear me?" she asked.
"I'm your grandmother."
"Yes," said Baby.
"If you come out
I'll bake you a delicious banana cake."

"Waaaaa," cried Baby.
"I like my food here,
and I won't come out."

Mrs. Tracy's father came over.
He put his head
against his daughter's stomach.

"Baby, can you hear me?" he asked.
"I'm your grandfather."
"Yes," said Baby.
"If you come out
I'll take you for a fast ride in my car."

"Waaaaa," cried Baby.
"I like riding in Mama,
and I won't come out."

Then Baby went to sleep.

"What will we do?" they all asked.
But nobody had an answer.

Then Daddy came home.

He gave his wife a kiss.

He gave Laura a kiss.
And he gave Craig a kiss.

Then he gave
Grandmother and Grandfather kisses too.

"Ummm," they all said.

"Hey, what is going on?"
whispered Baby.
"I'm kissing my family," Daddy said.
"And here's one for you."

Then he put his head
against his wife's stomach
and kissed.

"I don't feel anything," said Baby.
"No, not yet," said Daddy.
"But you will, when you come out."

"HERE I COME!" yelled Baby.
"Wait! Wait!" yelled everyone.

Dr. Wells rushed over
and helped bring Baby to her family.

"Welcome," he said.
"Umm," thought Baby.
"Where's my kiss?"

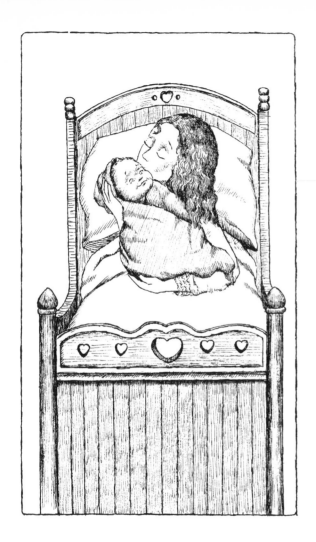

Mama kissed her.

Daddy kissed her.

Laura and Craig kissed her.   Grandmother and Grandfather kissed her.

"Umm," smiled Baby.
"I am staying right here."
Then she fell asleep in her mother's arms.

And that's the story
of Mr. and Mrs. Tracy,
Laura and Craig,
Grandmother and Grandfather,
and Baby—

who learned to walk
and talk

and paint yellow flowers—

but who always liked kissing best.